Harold and
the Duck

For Anno

First published in Great Britain in 2005 by Bloomsbury Publishing Plc
38 Soho Square, London, W1D 3HB

Text copyright © Bruce Robinson 2005
Illustrations copyright © Sophie Windham 2005
The moral rights of the author and illustrator have been asserted

Printed in China by WKT Printing Co Ltd

1 3 5 7 9 10 8 6 4 2

All papers used by Bloomsbury Publishing are natural, recyclable products made from
wood grown in well-managed forests. The manufacturing processes conform to the
environmental regulations of the country of origin.

Harold and the Duck

Bruce Robinson

and Sophie Windham

BLOOMSBURY
CHILDREN'S
BOOKS

Over the hills but not so very far away was Harold's Farm. There were yellow moons in the nights and woolly-meats in the meadows, a cobbled courtyard, and an old weather vane telling the wind which way to blow.

"I love everything about my farm," Harold used to say to himself. "Why, even the wind does exactly as it's told."

There was only one problem in Harold's life, and that was a stray cat.

This cat went by the name of Pud Pud. Pud was never allowed into the kitchen until Harold had gone to bed. The Pud didn't like it but sort of accepted it – it was part of the rules.

And so, on this particular night, all was apparently well. Pud had been fed and Harold was asleep in his basket. In the courtyard, silent but for the owls, starlight made silhouettes of the barns. And it was here, in the darkness of one of the corn bins, that something of consequence happened.

An egg was laid.

It was a pale egg with nothing very special about it, except that by dawn it had been abandoned by its mother and, by breakfast time, discovered by Harold.

"What has he got?" demanded Willow, who was a muddy little bloke with a pop-gun and big blue eyes.

"Obvious, isn't it?" said his sister, Lily. "Its mother's gone and I'm going to hatch it."

Within a very short while she had created a nest out of a colander and bobble-hat. Covering the egg with straw, she transferred her invention to the basement of a comfortable old Aga where the dishes usually warm.

"It's too hot in there, you'll cook it," said Willow.

"Well, we'll just wait and see, won't we?" said Lily.

And they did wait, and after a few days what they saw, or rather heard, was a tapping inside the egg. And then suddenly there was a crack, followed by a foot.

A small yellow face came out with eyes like a couple of match-heads. Expecting some sort of chicken, Harold blinked. This thing was the colour of a chicken, fluffy like a chicken, but it wasn't a chicken. It was a duck.

"Isn't he sweet?" said Lily. "I'm going to call him Duck."

Harold stood there wagging it till it nearly flew off, but barely got a pat.
He was a little miffed at all the attention this Duck was getting. Cuddles were
suddenly few and far between, going down and down as the Duck grew and
grew. It seemed to grow overnight, like a mushroom. In Harold's view it was a
horrible-looking bird, with a tuft of feathers on top of its head like part of a
toothbrush.

And worse, it slept in the kitchen with a lamp blazing over it to keep it warm. Nobody had considered the side effect of this, which was to keep Harold awake. No matter how he turned he couldn't nod, not even by smelling his special unwashed sock he'd had since he was a pup.

There was but one consolation. Within a week this Duck would be living outside with the rest of them and would be gone.

Two weeks later the Duck was twice the size and had taken over the entire kitchen, swaggering and quacking like it owned the place. There was no reasoning with it. It was self-centred, rude and arrogant.

It got corn for breakfast and flicked it all over the room. Not content with its own bowl, it got its beak into Harold's and threw his meat in the air. It was all too much and couldn't go on. Somehow this Duck must be made to go.

Next morning Harold had just finished his first session of barking in the yard and, as you can imagine, there were a lot of things that wanted barking at. Most of it was passing tractors and chicken-work, and sometimes too, of course, the Pud.

Now Pud Pud had been taking an interest in Harold's relationship with this Duck, and he was watching by the back door as the Wirey-One reappeared to find Duck standing in his water bowl like it was a pond.

"What are you doing in my bowl?"

"Quack."

"You arrogant Duck!"

Until now Harold had been unaware of the Pud.

"And there's that Vet's Bag of a cat!" he woofed. "Full of mice, and smirking!" He went after Pud like a bullet, out in the yard kicking dust to the barn.

Up the stairs they went

and down the other ones,

round and round the corn bins with Harold too puffed for threats.

Pud was a tail away, rushing into darkness, when Harold suddenly realised he'd been detained. His legs were still going but he wasn't going anywhere.

He was stuffed into an abandoned pipe like a cork.
Only his head stuck out, staring at the Pud who was
nonchalantly preening itself at the other side.

"Not like you to fall for an old trick like that, Harold?"

"Woof," said Harold.

"You know what you are?" said the Pud, with the kind of creamy smile
for which they are famous, "You are as dopey as the Duck."

"Woof," said Harold in exasperation.

"Oh, Woof to you," said Pud, mimicking
him. "Wuff, Wuff, Wuff. But it
doesn't get you anywhere,
does it? Do you think
I'd let a Duck get
the better of me?
I'd have that over-
grown Christmas
dinner out in a
second."

"How?" said Harold,
still bicycling with his
back feet.

"My advice, Harold, is when you're stuck, be it with a hole or a Duck, you'd better stop pushing and use your brains."

And with that, the Pud slunk away into a galaxy of buttercups. Harold woofed after him but gave up. And then gradually what the Pud said made sense. What if he stopped pushing and bicycled his feet in the opposite direction.

Suddenly he was out. He landed on the barn floor with a bump. He tried to think of something with his brain but it felt all sort of dopey. The only thing he could think about was how much he disliked the Duck.

Back at the house the kitchen was as messy as it had ever been, but Harold ignored it and tried to have it out, one to one, with the Duck.

He basically told him what's what, and who's who.

The Duck pecked him and got hold of his sock.

Now, as we know, this sock was of some importance to Harold, and he wanted it back.

Duck wanted to keep it and a row
broke out, and they both tugged
at either end of the sock, with
fur and feathers stuck up,
until Lily skipped in from
the garden.

"Oh, don't be so mean,
Harold," she said.
"You're much older
than him. Let him
have it."

The sock became the possession of
the delighted Duck and Harold
was ordered out of the house.
    "Bad dog," scolded Lily. "Bad,
bad dog."

Harold sat alone on the hill until the moon rose yellow as buttercups.

He was hoping the children would come and call him, but they hadn't.
It was approaching suppertime and he felt hungry. But more than that, he felt unwanted and sad. The unwantedness seemed to collect in his tail, which he couldn't lift no matter how he tried. His tail was as heavy as his heart.

At last hunger had the better of him, and with lifeless ears and a leaden wagger he made his way back to the house. The door was ajar and he crept into the kitchen behind so many sudden blinks he could hardly believe what he was looking at. There was a bowl of fresh food, fresh water, and no Duck.
A rapid sniff-round confirmed it. The Duck had gone!

Harold leapt into the air and came down in his basket. Oh joy, oh bliss, what a *present* is home! There, in all its magnificence, was a full meat serving, and he tucked in, savouring the texture of crunchy biscuits and rubbery morsels.

As he ate he became aware of laughter. It sounded like something funny was happening upstairs.

Although he wasn't really allowed, he felt happy enough to risk a telling-off and quietly climbed to the landing. The fun was coming from the bathroom, shrieks and splashes and Harold wanted to be part of it, and abandoning all caution he bounded in through the door.

The sight that greeted him wilted his wag. The children were sitting either end of the bath, with toys in between them which included the Duck! He was in the bath swimming in the bubbles, having a shampoo.

"You're not supposed to be upstairs," said Lily.

Harold knew where he wasn't supposed to be, where he no longer wanted to be –
and that was in the Duck's house. At the bottom of the stairs he saw a glint of
eyes in the darkness. It was Pud Pud waiting for his supper at the kitchen door.

"Aren't you going to chase me?" said the astonished Pud.

"No," said Harold, stealing past as though he wasn't there. "I'm leaving."

"Leaving?" said the Pud. "But where will you go?"

"That's not the sort of question you can put to a hound in my position," said Harold. "My mother came second at Crufts, and I will go where I'm wanted."

"Don't go, Harold. I shall miss you."

"Miss me?" said Harold with genuine surprise. "What would you miss about me?"

"Well, the Haroldness of you," said the Pud. "You're Harold, and this is your Farm. It won't be the same without you."

"It isn't the same anyway," replied the dejected dog, "and never can be."

Pud Pud watched him disappear, then turned to see the freshly-laundered and self-satisfied Duck waddle into the kitchen. The Pud knew he wouldn't have long before the children came down in their pyjamas, so without further ado he went in and made himself friendly with the Duck.

"Nice and warm in here, isn't it, Duck?" Paying no attention, the Duck got into Harold's basket.

"I should think," continued the Pud, "it's all to do with the coal on the fire in that very big oven?"

"Quack," agreed the Duck. He liked that lovely warm Aga. "That's my auntie," he said. "I was born in there."

"Really?" said the Pud, stretching the word as if it were an elastic band. "Well, did you know that ducks that come out of an oven, more often than not go back into one?"

"What are you talking about?" said the Duck.

"I'm talking about onions," confided the Pud. "I'm talking about potatoes. And I'm talking about gravy."

Pud was now whispering so close to the Duck's tuft that he could no longer be heard. But to judge from the bird's darkening expression the Pud was itemising all the common elements of a Sunday Roast, which naturally included sage and onion stuffing.

"What?" squawked the Duck. "Where do they stuff it?"

"Where I said they stuff it," said the Pud. "Most uncomfortable. I've seen it happen to dozens."

"Holy Quack!" said the Duck. "Let me out!"

Meanwhile, on the lane, Harold trudged in moonlight. It wasn't easy leaving home. He would miss the children, he would even miss the Pud.

He stopped to take a last look back at his beautiful Farm, but what he saw was somethin different to that expected.

There was a sudden screeching, then out of the darkness sped the tufted Duck. Its beak was wide and its feet a blur and it went past Harold like the fastest thing you can think of.

A moment later it was gone, squawking into the night as quickly as it had come.

There was a voice and Harold's ears instinctively lifted. The children were calling for him from far across the meadow. What could have happened to see that Duck off and make them want him back? The question was too complicated to answer, and anyway he didn't try, because he was already running for home.

Before he knew it he was in the kitchen. Round and round the table he ran, at least two and a half times, or more.

"Where were you?" said Lily. "We were worried about you." And scooping him up she smothered him in wonderful cuddles and wonderful kisses! And he ran round the table again.

"Woof! Woof! Woof!"

Harold was home, his wonderful home, with everything where it always had been. His bowl, his basket, his sock and his children. It was all wonderfully normal, and nothing to spoil it … except … except …

"There's that Vet's Bag of a cat!"
He hurtled after it like a torpedo, through the broccoli and across the yard, into
the barn and up the stairs and down the other side. He was barking and he was
happy. And Pud Pud was happy too.

The moon shone bright that night and everything was at peace. Woolly-meats slept in the pastures, and the weather vane stood still. Everything was as it should be, and all things as they always would be, on Harold's Farm.